CAMILA
THE STAGE STAR

written by ALICIA SALAZAR

illustrated by THAIS DAMIÃO

PICTURE WINDOW BOOKS
a capstone imprint

Camila the Star is published by Picture Window Books,
an imprint of Capstone.
1710 Roe Crest Drive
North Mankato, Minnesota 56003
www.capstonepub.com

Library of Congress Cataloging-in-Publication Data
Names: Salazar, Alicia, 1973– author. | Damião, Thais, illustrator.
Title: Camila the stage star / by Alicia Salazar; illustrated by Thais Damião.
Description: North Mankato, Minnesota : Picture Window Books, a Capstone imprint, [2021] | Series: Camila the star | Includes glossary, glossary of Spanish words, activities, and discussion questions. | Audience: Ages 5–7. | Audience: Grades K–1. | Summary: "When Camila tries out for a play, she practices hard to get ready for auditions. So she's extra disappointed when she doesn't get the starring role. But as she learns her part and works with the rest of the cast, Camila discovers there is more than one way to be a star"-- Provided by publisher.
Identifiers: LCCN 2020025173 (print) | LCCN 2020025174 (ebook) | ISBN 9781515882107 (library binding) | ISBN 9781515883197 (paperback) | ISBN 9781515891833 (pdf)
Subjects: CYAC: Acting—Fiction. | Theater—Fiction. | Hispanic Americans—Fiction.
Classification: LCC PZ7.1.S2483 Cb 2021 (print) | LCC PZ7.1.S2483 (ebook) | DDC [E]—dc23
LC record available at https://lccn.loc.gov/2020025173
LC ebook record available at https://lccn.loc.gov/2020025174

Designer: Kay Fraser

TABLE OF CONTENTS

Meet Camila and Her Family

Papá

Mamá

Ana, age 14

Andres, age 10

Camila, age 7

Spanish Glossary

actriz (ahk-TREES)—actress

anuncio (ah-NOON-syoh)—announcement

corazones (koh-rah-SOH-nehs)—hearts

estrella (es-TREH-yah)—star

increíble (eeng-kreh-EE-bleh)—incredible

Mamá (mah-MAH)—Mom

papel (pah-PEHL)—role

Chapter 1
A COMMUNITY PLAY

Camila bounced up and down as she read the colorful **anuncio**.

THE
**STAR
MUSICAL**
TRYOUTS
**SATURDAY
10am**

"If I got the lead **papel** in
the play, I would be a star!"
Camila threw her arms up.

Mamá agreed to take her to
the tryout.

Camila needed a scene to perform at her tryout. She chose her favorite part from *The Wizard of Oz*. It was the one where the Wicked Witch of the West goes to Munchkin land.

Camila practiced the words.
She practiced showing the
character's feelings.

She even watched herself in
the mirror to check the faces
she made.

By Saturday morning, Camila
could cackle just like the witch.

Chapter 2

THE TRYOUT

Finally, the day of the tryout arrived. Camila was ready.

But she couldn't help but feel nervous.

As she waited her turn, her heart pounded. Her legs shook. She kept forgetting part of her lines.

She checked her script and repeated: *my pretty, my pretty, my pretty.*

"Camila Maria Flores Ortiz," called the director. "They are ready for you."

"Please let me be the estrella!"
Camila thought. "Please let me be
the estrella!"

Camila stepped onstage.

She missed a word, but she kept going.

She forgot a wave, but she kept going.

She left out a turn, but she kept going.

When Camila stepped off the
stage, her shoulders slumped. "I'll
never be a star now," she said.

"You were **increíble**!" said
Mamá. "Don't worry!"

Camila waited. But the cast wasn't announced the next day.

Camila had to wait an entire week with her stomach in knots.

Finally, she and Mamá found the results online.

"I got the sidekick **papel**!" Camila said. "I wanted to be the star!"

"Do you think a real **estrella** would give up now?" asked Mamá.

Camila sighed. "Maybe if I do a good job, I can be the star next time," she said.

She practiced the star's part along with her own, just in case.

Chapter 3
THE STAR

Camila went to rehearsals four times a week. She even smiled when she had to work with Freya, the lead **actriz**.

The night of the first performance the cast and crew were in a flurry.

"I can't do it," she heard Freya say. "I'll forget all of my lines!"

Camila nearly cheered.
"I know all of her lines!" she
thought. "I can be the star
tonight!"

She walked over to tap the
director on the shoulder.

But when her eyes fell on
Freya, she stopped. Freya's face
was covered in tears. She was
shaking.

"What if it were me?" Camila thought.

She walked over to Freya and put her hand on her shoulder.

"It's okay to be nervous!" she said. "You can do this! I'll help you."

"I thought you wanted my part," said Freya.

"I did," said Camila. "But I really want the show to be a success. That way we all win. Let me help you practice a bit."

"Thanks!" said Freya.

When the curtain went up, both girls acted their **corazones** out. The audience roared and clapped.

When the show was over, Freya got flowers during the curtain call. She handed them to Camila with a smile.

"You're the star tonight, Camila!" she said.

Make an Emotion Machine

Do you want to be an actor like Camila? Actors need to be able to show lots of different emotions. By making a "machine" of emotions, you can have pictures in your mind that will help you imagine feeling certain things.

WHAT YOU NEED
- paper
- something to write and draw with
- tape (optional)
- your imagination

WHAT YOU DO

1. Choose an emotion. For example, being nervous. Then write down things that make you nervous. Some examples might be thunder storms, getting in trouble at school, or staying overnight someplace new.

2. Draw a picture to go with each thing you listed. If they don't all fit on one piece of paper, add another sheet with tape.

3. When you are all done, you will have a "machine of nervous." Now when you are asked to act like you are nervous, you can think of the pictures from your machine, and it will be easier for you to show this emotion!

Glossary

character (KAYR-ik-tuhr)—the part an actor plays in a play, movie, or show

curtain call (KUR-tin KAWL)—the appearance of the performers at the end of a play, which allows the audience to applaud them

nervous (NUR-vuhss)—having uncomfortable feelings

performance (per-FOR-muhns)—a public presentation of entertainment such as a play or concert

rehearsal (ri-HURSS-uhl)—a practice for a play

scene (SEEN)—a part of a play where there is no change in setting or break in time

script (SKRIPT)—the written text of a play, movie, or TV show

sidekick (SIDE-kik)—in stories, the person who helps or supports the main character

success (suhk-SESS)—a good outcome

Think About the Story

1. How did Camila get ready for the tryout? Was there anything else she could have done to prepare?

2. How did Camila feel when she saw the results? What clues in the art tell you how she felt?

3. Write a paragraph to describe how you think the performance went.

4. List five words that describe Camila. Then chose one of the words and use it in a sentence.

About the Author

Alicia Salazar is a Mexican American children's book author who has written for blogs, magazines, and educational publishers. She was also once an elementary school teacher and a marine biologist. She currently lives in the suburbs of Houston, Texas, but is a city girl at heart. When Alicia is not dreaming up new adventures to experience, she is turning her adventures into stories for kids.

About the Illustrator

Thais Damião is a Brazilian illustrator and graphic designer. Born and raised in a small city in Rio de Janeiro, Brazil, she spent her childhood playing with her brother and cousins and drawing all the time. Her illustrations are dedicated to children and inspired by nature and friendship. Thais currently lives in California.